1st

2nd

3rd

4th

5th

1st

2nd

3rd

4th

5th

1st

2nd

3rd

4th

For all the wonderful little dancers...
there's nothing little about the light you shine.

Imprint, A part of Macmillan Publishing Group, LLC
175 Fifth Avenue, New York, NY 10010

About This Book
The illustrations were hand drawn and digitally colored. The display type is Cochin LT.
The book was edited by Erin Stein and designed by Natalie C. Sousa. The production was supervised by
Raymond Ernesto Colón, and the production editor was Alexei Esikoff.

Our books may be purchased in bulk for promotional, educational, or business use.
Please contact your local bookseller or the Macmillan Corporate and Premium Sales Department
at (800) 221-7945 ext. 5442 or by e-mail at MacmillanSpecialMarkets@macmillan.com.

Imprint logo designed by Amanda Spielman
First edition, 2018
1 3 5 7 9 10 8 6 4 2
mackids.com

You can borrow, read, and dance away, but do not steal this little book of ballet!

The Little Dancers
Showtime!

by Maryann Macdonald   illustrated by Mandy Sutcliffe

{Imprint}
MAKE YOUR MARK

New York

"Who wants to be in a show?" asks Miss Amy. "It's called the Butterfly Ball."

"I do!" cries Jess, T W I R L I N G across the floor.

"Me, too," says Cara, already planning what her wings will look like.

Ollie swings Rosa, the littlest dancer, high into the air. "Look, Rosa's FLYING!"

"Will there be parts for all of us?" Emma asks.

"Everyone will shine at the Butterfly Ball," Miss Amy says with a smile.

"Imagine how a butterfly would dance. Practice at home and next week we'll dance for each other, just for fun."

"Butterflies are so beautiful,"
Rosa says to Emma. "I can't wait to be one."

"You would make a sweet butterfly," Emma says.
"But shows take lots of practice."

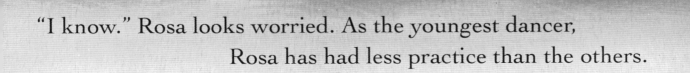

"I know." Rosa looks worried. As the youngest dancer,
Rosa has had less practice than the others.

"We'll help you," says Emma.

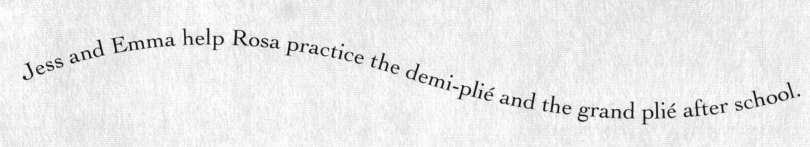

Jess and Emma help Rosa practice the demi-plié and the grand plié after school.

Ollie and Cara teach Rosa how to make
sad, ANGRY, shy, and **happy** faces
to show the audience her feelings.

When Rosa makes a dragonfly face, Ollie runs away.

Rosa practices her butterfly dance whenever she can.

She shows her happy face and keeps her back straight
and her head up, and she ends her dance with a STAR JUMP.

The next day, Rosa draws a picture of herself in a butterfly costume.
It looks just the way she wants to look in the show.

"I like how you decorated your wings,"
Cara says when she sees Rosa's drawing.

Rosa beams with pride. She knows Cara is a real artist.

When class starts, Miss Amy asks everyone to sit in a circle.
"Now we'll do our butterfly dances," she says.

Jess can't wait to show everyone her pirouette.

She SPINS around so FAST, it makes Rosa dizzy.

Ollie impresses everyone with his sautés and landings.

Calm and confident, Emma finishes by balancing on one foot without wobbling at all.

Cara's movements are so expressive, Rosa almost believes that Cara IS a butterfly.

At last, it's Rosa's turn. She closes her eyes and tries to remember her dance. She can see it in her mind so well that she forgets to open her eyes before she begins.

No one should ever dance with her eyes closed! Rosa trips and F A L L S.

Emma runs over. "Are you hurt, Rosa?"

Rosa shakes her head, but she rubs her knee.

Cara pokes her finger in the hole in Rosa's tights to tickle her.

"Everyone makes mistakes," she says. "It doesn't matter."

Then Miss Amy announces the parts for the Butterfly Ball.

"Jess, Cara, and Emma will be butterflies.

Ollie will play the cricket.

Rosa, you will be our glowworm."

A WORM? thinks Rosa. A SLIMY OLD WORM?

Ollie puts his hand on Rosa's shoulder. "Welcome to the ugly bug club," he says.

When class ends, Miss Amy puts her arm around Rosa. "The ballet begins and ends with the glowworm, you know," she says. "It's a very important part."

Rosa doesn't answer.

At home, Grandma Gardinia has spaghetti and meatballs waiting.

Rosa sits down to eat, but a few tears plop into her spaghetti.
"What's the matter, carissima?" Grandma asks.
Rosa tells her the whole story. Grandma listens.

"Once," Grandma says, "I was in a show, too. It was *Alice in Wonderland.* My friend was chosen to be Alice. Guess what I was."

"What?" asks Rosa.

"The TEAPOT," says Grandma.
Rosa giggles. Grandma giggles, too.
They laugh until Rosa's sadness slips away.

After dinner, Rosa practices CARTWHEELS.

It isn't quite dark when she sees Emma
coming up the street, holding something in her hands.

"I brought you a present," she says, and gives Rosa a jar.
Inside is an insect, shining with a spooky blue-green light.
"It's not a butterfly," explains Emma, "but isn't it beautiful?"

"Yes, Emma," says Rosa. "It is."
She opens the jar, tilts the little insect into the grass, and it crawls away.

"Good-bye, glowworm!" calls Emma. And Rosa blows it a kiss.

The little dancers have to learn all the steps for the show in just a few weeks.
Everyone wants to be perfect.

"Miss Amy wants me to do a cartwheel at the end, but I just can't!" Jess tells Rosa.

"I'll help you," Rosa promises, and she does.

Cara makes a garland for Rosa's hair and ties silvery streamers around a flashlight for Rosa to hold up as she leads everyone onstage.

When Rosa tries on her sparkling tutu, she feels

as beautiful as the butterflies...

and maybe more special.

On the night of the Butterfly Ball,
everyone is nervous, but it doesn't show.

Ollie's leaps are long, and Cara's and Emma's fluttering is fabulous.

Jess wows everyone with a PERFECT cartwheel.

But of all the little dancers, Rosa steals the show.
She is the first glimmer of light on the dark stage at the beginning

and the small bright spark leading all the dancers away at the end.

When everyone else has left the stage, Rosa turns and winks at the audience, and her light blinks off.

The audience EXPLODES into applause.

"I want the show to last forever!" Rosa says afterward in the dressing room.

"Don't worry," says Miss Amy. "We'll have many more performances.
But what a beautiful beginning!"

And Emma, Cara, Jess, Ollie, and Rosa all agree.

1st

2nd

3rd

4th

5th

1st

2nd

3rd

4th

5th

1st

2nd

3rd

4th